Chris Higgins

Illustrated by Lee Wildish

For baby Jake.
Welcome to *my* funny family.

Chapter 1

Dontie, V, Stanika, Jellico, Mum, Dad and I are going on a summer holiday. We're going to Cornwall on the train.

It'll take us nearly a whole day to get there and when we do, we're going to stay for a whole fortnight.

We're going to sleep in a tent in a farmer's field. Dontie found the campsite on the internet.

The place where we're staying is called Sunset Farm. It's on the edge of a cliff overlooking the Atlantic Ocean. At the bottom of the cliff is a wide sandy beach and there's a track down to it from the farm.

I'm so excited, I can't wait.

My best friend Lucinda is going to the Continent with her mum and dad.

At school we look up the Continent in the big atlas in the library but we can't find it anywhere.

'That's because it's abroad,' says Lucinda.

'I thought atlases showed everywhere in the world,' I say, puzzled.

'Not the Continent,' explains Lucinda. 'It's special. Dad says it's going to cost the earth.'

Lucinda's dad knows how much things cost because he's an accountant.

My dad's an artist.

We look up Cornwall instead and find out that it's at the very end of England, as far as you can go.

'We're going here,' I say and point to the bit at the bottom. 'The big toe.'

'The bunion,' says Lucinda and we both giggle. Lucinda's gran has got a bunion on her big toe.

'Mind you don't fall off the edge,' Lucinda adds and I giggle again to show that I can see the joke.

But then, of course, it starts me off. Worrying.

I'm Mattie Mind-a-lot.
Wendy Worry-worm.
Franny Fret-a-while.
Brenda Brood-a-bit.
Aggie Agonizer.

Florrie Fluster.
Tessie All-of-a-Tizz.
Penelope Panic-pants.
Stella Stressling.

These are some of the names my brother Dontie calls me.

Dontie is 11 and I am 9.

I don't think the last four are fair because it makes me sound like I make a fuss out loud.

I don't. I worry silently.

My sister V, who is 7, makes a fuss out loud about lots of things. Especially school.

I've got a little brother Stan who is 4 and a little sister Anika who is 2, as well. They're always together so we call them both by the same name, Stanika. It's easier.

My mum is called Mona and she's having another baby. At Christmas.

From a distance she looks like a teenager with her high ponytail. Close-up she looks a bit tired. Her tummy's starting to get fat because the baby's growing inside it but she can still get into her jeans. Just.

My dad is called Tim. He's tall and thin with a soft tickly beard that goes right round his chin from ear to ear.

Mum and Dad are quite young, not like Lucinda's parents.

Grandma says, 'They're far too laid-back, those two.'

Grandma is Dad's mum.

Granddad is Dad's dad.

Uncle Vesuvius is Mum's foster-dad. He's very old.

Jellico is our dog.

Now you know my whole family.

Grandma also says, 'Mattie's got an old head on young shoulders,' which is funny if you think about it.

But she doesn't mean I've got a head like hers with permed, grey hair and a face sprinkled with wrinkles, on a nine-year-old body.

She means I do all the worrying for the whole family.

Which is definitely true.

Someone's got to.

I add my new worry to Today's Worry List.

 DON'T LET ANYONE FALL OFF THE EDGE WHEN WE'RE ON HOLIDAY.

Chapter 2

We are on the platform waiting for the train to arrive and we are all carrying something, even Stanika.

Mum has a massive suitcase, stuffed full of clothes for us all. Plus a small bag with extra things for Anika.

Dad has a massive bag stuffed full of camping equipment.

Inside Dad's bag are:

1 gas stove
1 kettle

2 big saucepans
1 frying pan
7 plastic plates
7 plastic bowls
7 plastic mugs
7 knives, forks and spoons
Kitchen knives and ladles
and stuff
A torch
A big box of matches
And a big rug to sit on.

The bag is so heavy that no one but Dad can pick it up. Not even Dontie.

Plus, Dad has got an enormous tent to carry as well.

Each of us, even Stanika, has got our own backpack with a sleeping bag and a pillow rolled up on top. Inside our packs we've got food and drink for the journey, sweets from Uncle Vesuvius and surprises from Grandma to keep us occupied all the way down to Cornwall.

The train is late. We are investigating our surprises.

Dontie has got some Manga comics. 'Cool, Grandma!' he says, through a mouthful of liquorice allsorts.

I've got a brand new notebook and pen to use for my holiday. And sherbet lemons from Uncle Vez.

Stanika have got drawing books and felt tip pens. They're munching jelly beans.

V has got a book called *Cornish Myths and Legends*. I think Grandma has forgotten V doesn't like reading. She flicks through the pages looking at the pictures then she puts it aside to open the big bag of fruit pastilles Uncle Vez gave her.

As well, Dontie is carrying a sports bag

full of stuff he can't live without for a fortnight and is holding Jellico on the lead.

I'm in charge of Mum's handbag. It's got all our money and our tickets in it.

'I can depend on Mattie to look after it properly,' said Mum.

This worries me a bit.

In fact, this worries me a lot.

V is clutching a big bag full of beach games.

Stan is clutching Anika.

Anika is clutching Doggit.

Doggit is Anika's scruffy brown bedtime bear. Only he's not a bear. He's more half-dog half-rabbit.

That's why he's called Doggit.

'Put those things away,' says Mum. 'The train will be here soon.'

But Dontie's lost in his comic and V's munching her way through fruit pastilles.

When the train arrives, Jellico jumps up and down and barks a lot. People frown. Then he tries to run away.

'He's scared!' I explain, but no one listens.

'Tie him up a minute, Dontie, and give me a hand with this luggage,' says Dad who's puffing a bit.

'Get on the train the rest of you,' says Mum. 'V! Put those sweets away now or we'll go without you!'

V jumps off the bench and leaps on the train.

Then she leaps back off again.

'Where are you going?' shrieks Mum.

'I forgot the beach games,' says V.

Dad and Dontie struggle to lift the camping bag onto the train.

'Hurry up!' yells Mum, as the guard looks at his watch. 'Get on, Dontie!'

Dad pushes and Dontie pulls. One mighty shove from Dad and Dontie falls over backwards with the tent on top of him. It's on at last. Dad jumps on after it and slams the door. The whistle blows and we're off.

We make our way down the train in a Butterfield family procession. I feel a bit like the Queen. We have to keep stopping because passengers see Anika and Doggit and smile and want to talk to them.

Behind us, V keeps dropping bats, balls,

frisbees, buckets and spades. The balls roll right down the carriage.

Behind her, Mum drags her massive case.

Behind her, Dad and Dontie haul and heave and yank and tug the tent and the camping stuff down the aisle between them.

At last we find our seats. Dad shoves the tent and the big cases in the luggage store at the end of the carriage and everything else in the rack above our heads. Then he picks Anika up and pretends to stuff her in the rack too and everyone in the carriage laughs.

'Phew!' says Mum as she sinks into her seat. 'We made it! Let's hope we haven't forgotten anything.'

'I've got your handbag, Mum.'

'Good girl,' she says. 'I knew I could count on you.'

'I remembered the beach games!' says V quickly.

'Good girl,' repeats Mum and V smiles proudly.

Mum leans over and tickles Anika's tummy. 'And you remembered Doggit, clever girl.' Anika giggles and we all sit there, beaming at each other.

Except for Stan who's gone very quiet. Even for Stan.

'What's up, Stanley?' says Dad.

'Where's Jellico?' he asks.

Chapter 3

Everyone falls silent.

'Oh flip!' says Dontie. His face looks white.

I burst into tears. 'It's all my fault!' I wail.

'Why?' asks Mum, bewildered.

'I didn't think ... I should have thought ... I should've made a Worry List!'

'Don't be silly,' says Mum. 'This is nothing to do with your Worry List, Mattie.'

'It's Dontie's fault,' says V.

'No it's not!' says Dontie automatically.

'Yes it is. It was your job to look after him! I was looking after beach games, Mattie was Mum's handbag, you were Jellico,' points out V.

Dontie goes red. 'But Dad said to tie him up. And then I had to help him with the tent stuff. And then...' His voice trails away and he looks like he's going to cry too.

Anika crawls onto Stan's lap and Stan disappears from sight except for two hands clasped round her middle.

'It's nobody's fault,' says Dad firmly. 'Stop crying, Mattie.'

'But he'll starve to death under the bench with no food for a fortnight,' I sob. 'And he'll be so scared...'

'Phone Uncle Vez,' says Mum. Dontie, glad to be useful, delves inside his backpack for his mobile and hands it to Dad. Even from here I can hear Uncle Vez's rusty old cackle, more of a cough than a laugh. It makes me feel better.

'No problem,' says Dad, snapping Dontie's phone shut. 'He's on his way to rescue him.'

'Like Superman,' says Mum. But even the thought of Uncle Vez clad in a red cloak and red boots and red pants over his blue tights can't make me smile.

'Don't worry, Mattie, he'll be safe now,' says Mum. 'Uncle Vez will look after him for us.'

Dontie looks relieved.

'So Jellico can't come on holiday?' I ask in a small voice.

Mum shakes her head. 'Not this time.'

'Jellico's going to be sad without us.' Stan's voice, coming from somewhere behind Anika, sounds hollow.

Stan's right. Jellico was so looking forward to going on holiday. There would be beaches to run on, sea to play in, rabbits to chase. We'd told him all about it and he'd listened hard, head held to one side, soft brown eyes blinking, tongue dangling from the side of his mouth, hanging on to every word.

He would miss us so much.

A lump appears in my throat. I am just about to start crying again when I see Dontie biting his lip and staring out of the window, his shoulders hunched over with guilt.

So instead, I reach inside my backpack for my new notebook and pen. On the very first page I print in big, bold letters:

WORRY LIST

Then I write:

 Will Jellico chew through his lead and run after the train to try and catch up with us before Uncle Vez gets there to rescue him?

 If Uncle Vez gets there in time, how will Jellico cope for two whole weeks without us?

3 Or will he have forgotten all about us by the time we get home?

Chapter 4

When you go to Cornwall on the train, the tall grey city buildings give way first to houses with gardens, then to green fields with cows and sheep, then to the seaside. It's a long, long, long, long way.

At last, just when you think you will never arrive, you come to a big, high bridge and the train goes over it and you can look out of the window and see hundreds of boats on the river below.

Behind you is the whole of England,

Wales and Scotland.

In front of you is Cornwall.

Even after we've crossed the bridge into Cornwall it takes a long, long time for the train to get down to the very end. To the toe. To the bunion.

'Two more hours,' Mum says. 'Then we'll be there.'

'Two hours! That's 120 minutes! That's 7,200 seconds!' says V, who's good at maths.

According to V's book, Cornwall is a magic kingdom separated from the rest of the world by a big moat, and it's full of giants and mermaids and strange little goblin-like creatures. I read bits out loud to the others.

'That's stupid!' says V and rolls her eyes.

Stanika fall asleep.

So do Mum and Dad.

So instead I read Dontie's Manga comics, then I finish off my sweets, then I play noughts and crosses with V, then I sing 'Ten Green Bottles', 'Wheels on the Bus' and 'We Do Like to Be Beside the Seaside' with Stanika because by now they've woken up, and then I write more things to worry about in my new book.

This is what I add to my Worry List.

 Will Uncle Vez remember to water our vegetables every night?

 Will we have lost anything else by the time we get there, e.g. the beach games? The tent? Stanika?

6 Will we be able to find Sunset Farm?

 7 Will we manage to put the tent up? (I heard Dad discussing this with the man he bought the tent from and it didn't sound very easy.)

 8 Do I send Lucinda's postcard to her house or to the Continent?

What shall I do next?

'How much longer, Mum?'

Mum wakes up and looks at her watch.

'Another hour, Mattie,' she says and goes back to sleep.

'How many seconds in an hour?' I ask V.

'Sixty times sixty ... 3,600,' she says without a blink. I start counting.

Backwards.

Then I fall asleep.

And when I wake up, we are nearly there!

And now it is really magical, because you can see an island out in the sea and on that island is a castle! Stanika, V and I press our faces to the window.

'Is that where we're going?' asks V, excited.

'No, I don't think so,' says Mum, sifting through the information she's been sent. 'I don't think it's anywhere near as grand as that. I wonder what that island is called?'

'That's St Michael's Mount,' says an old lady, plump as a muffin with eyes like blueberries, sitting the other side of the aisle with her husband. They remind me of Aunty Etna and Uncle Vesuvius. Aunty

Etna died three years ago and now Uncle Vez lives alone and smokes pens instead of cigarettes.

The old man's eyes twinkle at Stanika and V. 'They say a giant lived there, back along.'

'Is he still there?' asks Stan.

'There's no such thing as giants,' scoffs V.

'Is that right?' says the old man and raises his eyebrows, like V doesn't know what she's talking about. 'Well, that's as maybe. All I know is what I've been told.'

'What have you been told?' persists V.

'Don't pester the gentleman,' says Mum, smiling. 'Come on V, get your things together. We're almost there.'

But no one wants to budge until we've heard the story, not even Dontie.

Chapter 5

'Long time back there was a giant called Cormoran,' explains the old man. 'He was a bad 'un. Many's the time he'd wade ashore and steal cows and sheep from the farmers round here. Eat 'em for his breakfast he would, with a couple of fried eggs and a few mushrooms. Folks got fed up with him in the end.

'One day, a brave lad called Jack came up with a plan. He rowed out to the island in the dark and dug a deep pit while

28

Cormoran was fast asleep. Then, when the sun came up, he blew a loud horn, right in the giant's ear.

'Cormoran woke up with a big angry roar and sprang up and chased after Jack. But he was blinded by the sun and, next thing, he'd fallen head-first into that blooming pit, and that was the end of him.'

'Yeah, right!' says V but now she doesn't sound so sure.

Stanika stare at the old man, round-eyed.

'Did he die?' asks Stanley sadly.

'No, my love,' says the old lady, and her voice is as warm and comforting as hot chocolate. 'It's just a silly old legend. Don't you take no notice of him and his silly tales. Alfred, you'll give these children nightmares!'

'What's a legend?' asks V.

'A fairytale.'

'See? I knew you'd made it up!' says V triumphantly. 'It's a good story though,' she admits.

'Oh, I didn't make it up,' says Alfred. 'Been around a long time, that story.'

'Longer than us!' says the old lady.

'My word, nothing's been around longer than us,' says Alfred and they laugh together. It sounds just like the clattering football rattle Uncle Vez has still got from the olden days and we all join in, we can't help it.

We'd better get off this train,' says Dad, collecting our luggage together, 'before it takes us home again.'

'Where are you staying?' asks Alfred.

'Sunset Farm,' says Dad. 'Trevowan.'

'Get the No. 7 outside the station. It'll take you the best part of an hour to get there.'

Mum groans. 'I didn't think it was that far!'

We get off the train and this time Dad goes to find a trolley and we load everything on to it and put Stanika on top. Soon we are sitting outside on our bags, waiting for the bus and eating biscuits. Around our feet seagulls hunch their backs and squawk angrily at each other as they fight over our crumbs.

'I can smell the sea,' says V.

'I can taste it,' I say in surprise, licking
my lips.

'It's the salt in the air,' explains Mum.
'Dear me, I'm exhausted. I can't wait to
get my head down.'

'Won't be long now,' says Dad.

A rusty old banger of a car pulls out of the car park and comes to a stop beside us. Alfred winds the window down and his wife leans over and waves to us. 'Have a nice holiday,' she says.

'Thank you!' we chorus.

'Say hello to my old mate Ted for me,' says Alfred.

'Who's Ted?' asks Dontie.

'Owns Sunset Farm. He knows a few stories. Get him to tell you about the Cornish piskies and the spriggans.'

'And the knockers,' says his wife.

'What's the knockers?' asks V, but it's too late, Alfred and his wife are off, lurching into the main road, smoke escaping from their exhaust.

'They're in your book, V,' I say, pulling

it out of my bag. She'd left it behind on the train.

'Oh those,' she sniffs. 'They're boring.'

Mum rolls her eyes at Dad and shakes her head. She gets cross at V because she won't read.

And then, the next thing, the bus is here and we all pile on.

Chapter 6

The No. 7 bus trundles slowly up through the lopsided town. On one side of the road the shops are at ground level but on the other side they're perched up high and you have to climb up steep steps to reach them.

'How would you manage those with a buggy?' remarks Mum.

'Look!' I cry. 'There's a bookshop called The Edge of the World!'

I remember my worry. **DON'T LET ANYONE FALL OFF THE EDGE.**

But we're not quite at the edge yet. The bus moves on, out of town and into the country.

It wends its way along the narrow, winding road which is separated from fields of cows by a stone wall smothered in moss and leaves and sprinklings of little flowers. The grey stone peeks through in places, like a face peering through an untidy fringe.

There's hardly anyone about.

Every so often a car coming the other way pulls into the hedge to let us pass.

Sometimes our bus driver waves and drives on past.

Sometimes he stops and leans out of his window to have a chat with the car driver.

Mum sighs.

A lady gets off by an old chapel.

A man gets off by a pub.

A mother with a baby in her arms gets off by a row of small cottages.

Everyone waves goodbye.

Soon there's just us and the driver left on the bus.

'Won't be long now,' says Dad and rubs Mum's back for her.

But then the bus slows down to a snail's pace.

'What now?' says Mum.

A tractor has pulled out of a field in front of us, just at the bottom of a steep hill.

'Bad timing!' says Dad.

'No rush, is there?' says the bus driver.

'Not really,' says Dad. 'We're on holiday.'

'Thought so.'

'Just so long as we're in time to put our tent up before it gets dark,' says Mum.

'Relax, Mrs,' says the driver. 'You're on Cornish time now.'

'What's Cornish time?' asks V.

'All the time in the world,' he says and stops for a chat with another driver.

'Oh dear,' says Mum weakly and shifts uncomfortably in her seat. 'Now I can see why it takes so long to get here.'

Poor Mum. I think it's hard to sit still for a long time with a baby in your tummy.

The driver starts the bus again and points to the tractor disappearing over the hill in front of us. 'He's going your way.'

'To Sunset Farm?' asks Dontie.

'Aye. That's Ted, going home for his supper.'

He teases the bus gently up the hill and it starts to wheeze and gasp. At last, at the top, it comes to a spluttering, shuddering stop. I glance anxiously at Mum who has closed her eyes and is mouthing some words to herself.

Actually, I'm quite good at lip-reading. I'm glad she's not saying those words out loud.

'Has it broken down?' asks Dontie.

'Be all right in a minute. Always does this. Pretty, ain't it?'

We all stand up to see and now it's our turn to gasp. It looks like a beautiful picture painted by Dad, using every single colour on his palette.

Spread in front of us is a patchwork of green, brown and yellow fields, dotted with black and white cows, with the road running right down through it like a silver ribbon, all the way to the cliff edge.

Beyond it lies the Atlantic Ocean, grey as a gun.

Above it is a livid purple, crimson and blue-streaked sky, with a fiery red ball of sun poised to fall out of it into the

steel-grey, seal-grey, sea.

Silhouetted against the setting sun near the cliff edge, is a big wheel and a tower with a chimney stack.

'What's that? A fairground?' asks Dontie hopefully.

'That's the old tin mine. There was a big disaster there about a hundred years ago. It closed down a few years back.'

Next to the tin mine, near the cliff edge, is a collection of farm buildings with one or two tents scattered around.

'Is that it?' I ask. 'Is that Sunset Farm?'

'That's it!' says the driver and he lets the handbrake off to freewheel down the hill, gathering speed as we go. Mum's eyes whip open in alarm as we all whoop with delight.

We've arrived at last!

Chapter 7

I love it here at Sunset Farm. We've only been here two days and I feel as if I've lived here for ages.

I wish I *did* live here.

Mum wasn't sure at first.

When she saw the kitchen area she said, 'It's a bit basic!'

When she saw the showers she said, 'It's a bit primitive!'

When she saw the toilets she said something very rude indeed.

Then Dad had a little trouble putting up the tent. A lot of trouble actually.

And V said she wasn't going to sleep in it anyway because she'd seen a spider.

And Dontie said there was nothing to do here.

And Mum discovered she'd left Anika's bag of stuff on the bus.

And then it started raining.

'That's it!' Mum said. 'First thing in the morning, we're going home.'

It was like all my Worry List come true.

But then a fish and chip van came round and we had our tea inside the tent, which Ted had managed to get standing up straight instead of crooked. I liked it with the rain drumming down on the canvas and us nice and dry inside.

Then Dad dug out Stanley's spare pair

of Buzz Lightyear pyjamas for Anika, which fitted her beautifully, and he tucked her and Stanley into their sleeping bags, next to each other. Then he tucked Mum into her sleeping bag next to them.

'Can I go to bed?' said V who was dying to get into her brand new sleeping bag too.

'I've got an idea,' said Dad. 'Why don't

we all go to bed?' and so Dontie, V, Dad and I climbed into our sleeping bags and, just for once, we didn't bother with teeth, because it was still pouring with rain.

We all lay down in a line, with Stanika in the middle, Mum next to Anika, V next to Mum, me next to V and, on the other side, Dad next to Stanley and Dontie next to Dad.

'Like a tin of pilchards!' said Dad, which made us all giggle.

Then we went off to sleep in the tent which was warm and snug and smelt of salt and vinegar, while the rain beat down outside.

And in the morning it had stopped. The day was bright and sunny and we had breakfast on the grass – which was still a bit wet – and Ted brought us some new-laid eggs from the hens that were pecking round the farmyard. After a while the bus came freewheeling down the hill and the driver got out and handed Mum Anika's bag of stuff.

'Left it on the bus, you did,' he said.

'I know,' said Mum. 'Thank you.'

'Nice day,' he said.

'Yes, it is,' said Mum and went off to

give the toilets a good clean.

After that we went down to the beach.

By the end of the day, Mum had forgotten all about going home.

Chapter 8

I like talking to Ted. He reminds me of Uncle Vesuvius. He's lived here for ages. All his life.

He was born at Sunset Farm and his father before him and his father before him and his father before him...

'Goes back to the seventeenth century, I think,' says Ted, taking his hat off to scratch his head.

Funny to think of a whole line of Teds stretching back into the past. All of them wiry and weather-beaten, with creased-up, crinkly eyes and big brown splodges on their arms from the sun.

And a whole line of Teds stretching forward into the future too. Ted has got three sons and three daughters, all grown-up now, and four little grandchildren including one called Ted.

'Three boys and three girls!' smiles Mum and strokes her tummy, thoughtfully. 'Like us, maybe.'

Ted studies her. 'Think you're right there. Looks like a boy to me.'

'How can you tell?' I ask.

'Practice. I always know if it's going to be a heifer or a bull calf.'

'I'm not a cow!' says Mum indignantly.

But now I know I'm going to have a baby brother.

'Ted might be wrong, Mattie,' says Mum later. 'You can't really tell by looking.'

Ted can.

Ted knows everything.

Ted knows how to milk cows by hand and make cheese.

Ted knows how to keep the hens safe from the wily fox.

Ted knows how to feed newborn lambs who've lost their mothers with milk from a bottle.

Ted knows the name of every single flower in the fields and hedgerows.

'What about the weeds?' says V.

'No such thing as a weed,' says Ted. 'A weed is just a flower in the wrong place.'

Ted is the wisest person I know.

He lets us feed the chooks with him.

The hens are called chooks because they make a chooking noise. So do we, when we feed them. We go, 'Chook, chook, chook, chook, chook,' as we walk across the yard and the chooks run after us, flapping their wings.

'Where's your wife, Ted?' I ask and then I wish I hadn't because he looks sad.

'She passed away.'

'Passed away' is a euphemism. We did it in Literacy. It's a nice way of saying she died.

Aunty Etna died.

Uncle Vez said she 'went to pastures new'.

Grandma said she 'went to a better place'.

Dontie said she 'kicked the bucket'.

These are also euphemisms.

'I worry about people dying,' I confess to Ted.

'Don't you waste your time worrying about that.'

'I can't help it. I worry about everything.'

I tell him about my Worry List.

'Why don't you give that old Worry List a rest while you're on holiday, Mattie?' he says and scatters corn around Stanika so the hens peck at their toes. Stanika both giggle.

'Tickles,' says Anika who says a new word every day.

'I can't.'

'Yes you can. Put it in that backpack of yours and forget about it.'

So I do. We make up a song about it.

It's like the one that Uncle Vez sings

called 'Pack up your troubles in your old kit bag'.

Only this one is called 'Pack up your worries in your old backpack'. It goes like this.

> Pack up your worries in
> your old backpack
> And smile, smile, smile.
>
> Pack up your worries in
> your old backpack,
> Forget them for a while.
>
> What's the use of worrying?
> It never was worthwhile.
>
> So pack up your worries in
> your old backpack
> And smile, smile, smile.

It's a great song. Soon we know all the words and do you know something?

It works. I'm not worried any more.

But there's still something I can't help wishing for.

I wish that Jellico was here as well.

He'd love it with us on Sunset Farm.

Chapter 9

'Ted!' V and I race towards the tractor as it trundles into the farmyard. 'Tell us about the Cornish piskies.'

'And the spriggans and the knockers?' asks V.

I'd been reading the Cornish myths and legends book to Stanika and V was ear-wigging, even though she says books are boring.

Ted gets down from his tractor and swings Stanley up to the driving seat.

'Me! Me!' squeals Anika so he puts her up there too.

'Why do you want to know about them?' he asks.

'Alfred said you'd tell us,' V says.

'Well, they're all part of the faery folk,' he says and sits himself down on the wall.

V and I settle down beside him. Dontie pulls a face and says, 'Faeries!' and carries on playing football with the hens.

But I can't help noticing he's ear-wigging too. And even Dad, who is painting a picture of Greta the pig, puts down his brush and listens to Ted.

'The piskies were friendly little faery folk who rode about on snails.'

'Snails!' says V, picking one up off

the ground and examining it. 'They must've been tiny!'

'They were,' agrees Ted.

'What were the spriggans?'

'Oh them,' says Ted pulling a face. 'Ugly little rascals. You don't want to know about them. They were bad 'uns.'

'Yes we do,' says Dontie, perking up. 'Tell us about the spriggans. Why were they bad 'uns?'

'They raised whirlwinds and storms to spoil the crops.'

'Is that all?' says Dontie, disappointed.

'No. They stole babies from their cradles too.'

'Wicked!' says Dontie approvingly.

Stanley puts his arm around Anika and pulls her closer to him.

Mum strokes her tummy protectively.

'It's only a story,' adds Ted quickly. 'It's not true.'

'Who were the knockers?' I ask, but now I'm not sure I really want to know. Maybe they were even worse than the spriggans.

'The knockers were little creatures who guarded the tin mines. Used to be lots of mines round here.'

'Were they bad 'uns too?' asks Dontie.

'Not if you shared your food with them,' says Ted. 'They'd look after you then. Miners would break off bits of their pasties for them.'

'Why?'

'To keep them safe in the mines. And farmers would make sure there was something left over for them at the end of the day.'

'Why?'

'So they would reap a good harvest. Always leave a bit of something out for the knockers, you would. Keep them on your side.'

'You leave something out for the knockers, don't you?'

'No,' Ted laughs.

'Yes you do, I've seen you. Every night, you put some food in the bowl by your back door.'

We all look over at the bowl. There's nothing in it now.

'Scraps for the dogs,' says Ted.

But I don't believe him.

That evening Dad and Dontie walk into town to buy pizza for us for a Friday night treat. They come back with a margherita, a ham and pineapple and a fiorentina, my favourite. Dontie and I share the fiorentina and this time it's my turn to have the fried egg in the middle.

But tonight, even though it's the best bit with the egg on it and it makes my mouth water just thinking about it, I hide the last slice in my sleeping bag.

Then, when it's dark and I'm sure everyone else is asleep, I get it back out.

I don't eat it.

OK, I do give it a tiny lick but that's all. Actually, it's a bit cold and leathery now, not very nice. Then I crawl on my tummy like a commando to the door of the tent.

And very, very slowly, so it doesn't make a noise and wake anyone up,

I unzip the bottom of the tent, just far enough to push the pizza through.

Then I make a wish.

The next morning, the pizza has gone.

Chapter 10

The beach below our campsite is brilliant. There is so much to do. When you first see it from the cliff top it looks deserted, but when you clamber down the path and start investigating, it turns out to be teeming with life.

There is always something new to investigate. The first thing you notice is the birds. Seagulls, nesting on the cliff-ledges, screech at each other all day long.

'Can I climb up to see them close?'

asks Dontie this morning when we all troop down to the beach.

'No,' says Dad. 'You'll disturb them. My goodness, did you see that? Look, there's another one!'

We all watch as a snow-white bird with black wing-tips dives like a dart into the sea. Then another one plummets like a lift down a shaft.

'I wonder what they're called?' says Mum.

'I think they may be gannets,' says Dad.

'Really?' I say in surprise. 'Like V?'

Sometimes Grandma calls V a gannet because she's greedy. I didn't know a gannet was a real thing.

'Ted would know what they are,' says Mum.

'Let's go and ask him!' I say, so V and

I climb back up the cliff path to find Ted.

He's cleaning out the pigpen. It stinks a bit so we don't offer to help, we just perch on the wall and fire questions at him while Greta roots around in the mud. Greta is named after Ted's favourite actress from the old black and white films, Greta Garbo, and she's pregnant too, like Mum. The pig, I mean, not the actress. I think she's dead.

Then we go back down to the beach.

'Ted says yes, the birds are gannets and they can see fish in the sea from 30 metres up,' I report.

'They've got good eyesight!' Dad's set up his easel for a day's painting.

'Ted says the seagulls are herring gulls and the babies beg for food by pecking at a red spot on their mum's beak.

Then their mums sick up their own food into their mouths.'

'Saves on all that shopping and cooking and washing up,' says Mum as she unpacks our picnic. 'I wish I was a flipping seagull. Come on, gannets! Lunchtime.'

Dontie has been exploring one of the big, dark caves that go deep into the cliffs.

'Ted says those caves go all the way back up to the old tin mine at the top of the cliffs,' I say as Mum hands me a cheese and tomato sandwich.

'You be careful,' says Mum. 'You might get lost inside.'

I don't want to play in the caves. They're dark and scary. I'd rather play in the rock pools with Stanika.

'Are you listening, Dontie?' asks Mum, but Dontie's got his mouth full. We sit on the beach munching our sandwiches.

'Ted says the shells that stick to the rocks are limpets and they are alive and feed on seaweed.'

'They're a bit like snails,' says Mum.

'Snails don't feed on seaweed,' Dontie points out.

'Ted says the Cornish piskies ride around on snails.'

'Does he now?' says Mum and she sounds a bit bored.

'Ted says if you look in the rock pools you might see tiny crabs or shrimps or a sea urchin or even a starfish.'

'You're a shrimp,' says Dontie to Stanley.

'You're an urchin,' says Stanley to Dontie and everyone laughs, even Anika, who's too young to get it.

Along the shoreline I notice big clumps of seaweed.

'Ted says you can tell what the weather's going to be like from seaweed. 'Ted says,

> If the seaweed's dry,
> the sun is out,
> If the seaweed's damp,
> there's rain about.

'Ted says...'

'Goodness me!' says Mum. 'Ted says a lot, doesn't he?'

'Only if you ask him,' I explain.

After lunch we go beachcombing. I write down the unusual things I find in my new book so I can ask Ted what they are. Dad sketches them for me alongside my notes.

These are some of the things I find:

1. A shell that looks like an ice-cream cornet
2. A blobby jelly thing
3. A shell that looks like a pasty
4. Some spongy things

I show them to Mum. 'That's nice,' she says then lies down on her back, turning her face towards the sun. Her tummy isn't flat like it used to be. The new baby is making it poke out a bit.

'Mmm,' she wriggles her toes happily. 'This is perfect.'

I lie down beside her and wriggle my toes too.

I love it here.

But Mum's wrong. It's not quite perfect.

It's like a cloud in the sky keeps blocking out the sun.

It's like my best ever picture which Lucinda flicked paint on by mistake.

It's like my 1,000 piece jigsaw of Australia with Ayers Rock missing.

Because something *is* missing. Something with soft brown eyes, scruffy hair and a waggy tail.

That's why I saved the best bit of pizza and put it outside the tent last night.

For the knockers.

If anyone can help me, they can.

Somewhere above us, a dog barks urgently. We all look up.

At the top of the cliff a small figure is waving and a big untidy dog is scrambling his way down the path, tail swishing madly from side to side like a hairy windscreen wiper.

It can't be.

I don't believe it.

It is!

'Jellico!' shrieks V and we all jump up.

It worked!

Chapter 11

Now Jellico is back with us we practically live on the beach. He loves it. He spends all day chasing seagulls and barking at the waves.

Uncle Vez said poor old Jellico was pining away for us. I knew he would be.

'Went right off his food, he did,' says Uncle Vez, puffing on his biro. 'He was missing you all.'

I was missing him too. Only now I've got him back, I'm missing Lucinda instead. But I haven't gone off my food.

I love it here on the farm. I love sleeping in the tent and feeding the hens and scratching Greta's back and I don't even mind the lukewarm showers and the dodgy toilets, though I won't go in them on my own in the dark.

But I miss someone to talk to, play with, a friend of my own. Brothers and sisters are OK, but they're not the same.

Everyone needs a friend. Even Uncle Vez has made one.

'Ages since I been to Cornwall,' remarks Uncle Vez. 'Might do a spot of fishing, now I'm here.'

'Come to the right place for that, boy,' says Ted, even though Uncle Vez hasn't been a boy for a long, long time.

Ted lends Uncle Vez a rod and a bucket

and Uncle Vez finds himself a nice rock
to sit on.

'He looks like a little
old gnome with
that fishing rod,'
observes Dontie
and Mum says,
'Sshhh! Dontie,
that's rude!'
but then I catch
her giggling at Dad.

'He won't catch anything,' Dontie says,
but he's wrong. Every time we clamber
over the rocks to see how he's getting on,
Uncle Vez has caught another fish! But
he only keeps the ones big enough to eat.
He throws the rest back into the sea.

Later on, Ted comes down to see how
he's doing. He peers in the bucket. 'Not

bad!' says Ted. 'For a beginner.'

Uncle Vez shifts his hat back on his head. There is a line where his hat's been. Above the line, his forehead is milky-white. Below the line, his face is fiery-red.

'Enough for a barbecue there, I reckon,' he says proudly. 'We'll have a barbie on the beach tonight.'

'Good idea,' says Ted. 'I'm partial to a bit o' mackerel myself.'

We gather driftwood while Dad searches out good stones to make a barbecue and Uncle Vez guts the fish. Jellico and the seagulls between them gulp down the scraps.

Mum nips up to town on the bus and comes back with a bag of bread rolls, a flagon of cider for the men, some orange juice for us and a huge chocolate cake for afters.

'It's getting dark,' says V, so Ted gets the fire started and soon it's red and glowing. The wood spits and crackles as the oil from the fish drips on to it. Long fingers of flickering light creep out over the soft, shadowy sand.

The fish doesn't take long to cook. 'Who wants a Big Mac-kerel Burger?' Dad asks as he scoops out pieces of fish for us from the fire and drops them onto the crusty bread. Mum hands one to me. I hesitate.

'What if I don't like it?' I ask worriedly.

'Try it and see,' says Mum.

I sniff it.

I lick it.

I nibble it.

I gobble the lot.

'It's delicious!' I say.

'The tastiest thing I have ever eaten in my whole life,' Mum agrees, licking her fingers.

'Tastiest and tangiest,' sighs Dad.

'Tastiest, tangiest and most tempting,' says Dontie.

'Tastiest, tangiest, most tempting and most tantalizing,' says Uncle Vez, catching on.

'The tastiest, tangiest, most tempting titbit to titillate and tantalize your tastebuds,' says Ted.

Wow! Ted's good at this.

No one can think of another t-word.

'You win,' says Uncle Vez.

Mum cuts the chocolate cake into big slabs and hands it around.

'What if I don't like it?' asks Dontie in a girly voice, pretending to be me.

'I'll eat it!' says Dad and whips it off him. Dontie jumps on his back and they wrestle until my brother manages to grab the cake back, now covered in sand, and stuff it into his mouth.

'You two!' says Mum, but she doesn't mean it.

It's magic here at Sunset Cove by the fire, under the night sky.

Above us, a bright, shiny moon hangs like a lamp from a ceiling of stars, lighting up the grey and silver sea. The waves lap gently on the shore.

I turn around. Towering behind us, the high cliffs lurk with their dark, hidden caves.

I shiver all over.

'Cold?' asks Mum and pulls me closer to her warm body.

'No.' But I stretch out my hands towards the heat of the fire.

'Someone walked over your grave,' says Ted and I stare at him in surprise before I glance back again over my shoulder.

'Don't worry, Mattie,' says Mum. 'It's just a saying! There's no one there.'

But she's wrong.

There was someone there.

A boy. I saw him. Near the caves.

He was watching us.

But now he's gone.

Chapter 12

During the night the wind comes up and then it starts raining. I can hear Uncle Vez snoring loudly in his little tent beside us. Outside, Jellico whines.

Dad gets up to let him in. I take cover in my sleeping bag as he shakes himself dry and then settles on my feet. No one else stirs. Dad goes outside to check everything is secure. I can see his torch through the tent and feel him banging the tent pegs hard into the ground.

'Blowing a gale out there!' he mutters to himself, when he comes back in.

'Will we be all right, Dad?' I whisper.

'Safe as houses. Back to sleep now.'

'Don't worry, Mattie,' comes Mum's sleepy voice. 'You're safe in here.'

I'm not worried. It's nice cuddled up inside the tent all together, with Jellico warming my feet like Grandma's electric blanket, while the rain lashes down outside.

But then I think of that boy watching us on the beach and I wonder if he's got somewhere to shelter from the rain. And though I know he must be tucked up in bed, nice and warm too, I start to worry after all.

In the end I sneak my writing book out of my backpack.

In the darkness I scribble:

WORRY LIST

 **Is that strange boy all right?**

And then at last I fall asleep.

In the morning, the skies are still grey. Ted brings over some fresh eggs for breakfast.

'What are you doing today?'

'I thought we might get a bus into town, do some shopping this morning,' says Mum.

Dontie pulls a face. 'Do we have to?'

'You can stay if you like,' says Mum. 'Look after Jellico.'

Dontie brightens up. Suddenly I say, 'Can I?'

Mum looks at me in surprise.

'Don't you want to look around, Mattie? Choose a few postcards? Buy some souvenirs?'

I feel torn.

I want to send a postcard to Grandma and Granddad and to Lucinda. I want to get them all presents.

But I want to go back down to the beach and check that the boy is all right.

'Let her stay if she wants to,' says Ted. 'I'll be here if she needs me.'

'I'll be around too,' says Uncle Vez.

'All right,' says Mum decisively. 'We won't be long.'

But they are long. They take ages just getting ready to go. And even then, I have to chase up to the bus stop after them because I spot Doggit has been left behind.

'I'm going to catch them up!' I shout to Ted and Uncle Vez who are chatting in the yard as I streak past.

Then I wait with the others 'til the bus comes. They all wave goodbye to me from the back window. When the bus is out of sight, I turn back to the farm, feeling very grown up on my own.

There is no sign of anyone. No Dontie, no Uncle Vez, no Jellico, no Ted. Just a few chooks, pecking hopefully for corn in the yard, a line full of washing and Greta rooting around in her pen.

Everyone's disappeared. That's weird.

Then it clicks. Ted and Uncle Vez must've thought I'd changed my mind after all and chased after the others to catch the bus into town.

For the first time in my life, I am alone.

I look up at the sky. It's still overcast. It looks as if it might rain again.

I don't care. I'm going down to the beach.

Chapter 13

The cove is deserted. Not a soul is in sight, not even a seagull.

The tide is out and the sand looks as if it's been washed clean by the rain. Even the rock pools seem empty, though I know they're not.

I look up at the cliffs. No gulls to be seen, swirling and shrieking. They must be up there on the high ledges, hiding in crevices, behind boulders, but everything is silent.

I'm completely alone in the world.

I don't like it.

But then, over by the entrance to the largest cave, I see something out of the corner of my eye. A boy.

It's him. The boy I saw watching us last night.

I wave and he turns to disappear back into the cave.

'Don't go!' I shout. 'Wait for me!'

He stops and stares at me, perfectly still.

'Do you want to play?' I call but he doesn't answer so I run over to him, coming to a stop about a metre away.

Close up I can see he's about my age, maybe a year or so older. He's skinny and brown, with untidy sun-streaked hair and he's wearing tatty old trousers rolled up to the knees. That's all.

'Have you been swimming?' I ask.

'Not today.' His voice is slow and rough.

'Do you live round here?'

'Up along.' His head jerks up to the top of the cliff, away from the farm, where a huddle of old cottages stand.

'What's your name?'

'Will.' He pauses, then he adds,

'You ask a lot of questions.'

'You don't.'

His face breaks into a grin and it's like the sun's come out. 'Cheeky mare. What you called?'

'Mattie.' I grin back. He's strange, but I like him.

'Got anything to eat?' he asks.

I shake my head. 'Are you hungry?'

'Always hungry, me.'

He looks it. I can see his ribs. I remember him watching us last night as we ate our barbecue and I feel a bit guilty now that I didn't tell Mum. She'd have given him something to eat.

Only last night I wasn't sure about him. He was a bit spooky, hiding there in the dark cave all on his own, watching us. I wasn't even sure if he was real or not.

I thought I might have imagined him. Mum's always saying I've got a vivid imagination.

Now I know he *is* real I wish I had something to give him. Then I have a brain-wave.

'Come on up to the farm,' I say. 'Ted'll give you something to eat.'

He shakes his head. 'I can't.'

'Why not?'

He shrugs.

I glance up and down the beach. Not an ice-cream hut in sight. 'There's nothing to eat here,' I say regretfully.

'Yes there is.'

'Where?'

He rolls his eyes like he can't believe how ignorant I am. 'Come on,' he says, 'I'll show you.'

Chapter 14

I thought Ted knew a lot.

Will knows even more than he does.

We squat down beside a rock pool and he lifts back strands of seaweed so we can peer underneath.

'You can eat this,' he says and breaks off a piece of seaweed for me to try.

It's really chewy.

'It tastes like the spinach we grow at home,' I say in surprise. 'But saltier.'

He nods and we munch away in silence,

companionably. Then he points to the limpets clinging tight to the rocks.

'You can eat these too,' he says and prises one off with a squelch.

'Ugh! No thanks!'

I watch in horror as he scoops the squashy bit out with his fingernail and sticks it in his mouth.

'It's alive!'

He chews quickly, swallows, then grins. 'Not any more, it ain't!' He digs another shell out of the sand. It's got something alive in it as well. I can see two little tubes waving about.

'What's that?'

'A cockle. They keep the beach clean, they do. See them?' He points to the two little tubes.

'Yeah.'

'They use them to suck up bits of dead plants and animals lying about in the sand.'

'Like little hoovers!' I say in delight but he looks at me blankly. Maybe they don't have vacuum cleaners in Cornwall.

Then he eats it.

We move from pool to pool and he shows me loads more stuff and tells me what everything's called.

He shows me mussels that cling to the rocks with tiny threads.

He shows me whelks that feed on the mussels.

He shows me hermit crabs that don't have a shell of their own so they move into other creatures' shells instead.

'Like cuckoos,' I say.

'Aye,' he repeats, 'like cuckoos.' And this time he looks at me as if I'm really clever instead of daft.

Every so often he'll lever something out of a shell and gobble it up. I think he must be starving.

'Try one,' he offers, 'they're good.'

But I shake my head because I don't like eating things that are alive. 'No thanks, I'll stick to the seaweed.' Then I add,

'I think I might be vegetarian.'

He looks at me puzzled again, as if he hasn't got a clue what I'm talking about.

Maybe they don't have vacuum cleaners or vegetarians in Cornwall.

I change the subject. 'Can you swim?'

His eyes light up. 'Course I can.'

'So can I.' I feel proud I can say this. I only learned to swim a few months ago.

He nods. 'I've seen you.'

'I'm not very good,' I admit.

'You're all right,' he says kindly. Then he adds, 'For a stickleback.'

I don't know what a stickleback is, but it sounds nice. I smile at him happily and he grins back.

'I bet you can swim like a fish,' I say.

'Like a silkie,' he says proudly.

'What's a silkie?'

But before he can answer, I hear my name being called.

'MATTIEEE!'

Dontie and Jellico have appeared around the headland.

'That's my brother. He's been exploring.'

Will narrows his eyes. 'Tell him to watch those tides,' he says.

I stand up as Jellico, with a joyful bark, bounds across the beach and knocks me flying as he tries to leap into my arms.

'Down boy!' I laugh and scramble back to my feet as Dontie runs up.

'What are you doing down here on your own?' he asks.

'I'm not on my own. I've been talking to Will.'

'Who's Will?'

I turn around to introduce him, but there's no sign of my new friend.

'He's gone,' I say, puzzled.

Jellico trots round and round in a trail, sniffing the sand. Finally he goes to the entrance of the cave and barks.

'Thought you'd gone to town with the others,' says Dontie and wanders into the cave to investigate. But Jellico doesn't follow him, he just stands there barking madly.

'Come out of there, Dontie!' I call and my voice echoes back at me, spookily. **DONTIE! DONTIE!** DONTIE!

'Why?' Dontie's voice is muffled from inside the cave.

'Mum said, don't go in there!' **DON'T GO IN THERE!**

'Scaredy-cat!' Dontie's voice is mocking,

but he comes back out. 'There's nothing in there.'

But my brother is wrong. Twice.

NUMBER 1.

I'm not a scaredy-cat.

A worry-guts, yes. A scaredy-cat, no.

NUMBER 2.

There *is* something in that cave.

Some*one*.

Will is hiding in there. Somewhere.

And I don't know why, but he doesn't want to be found.

Chapter 15

If anyone will know, Ted will.

'What's a silkie?' I ask him, next morning.

'Where did you hear that? A silkie's a seal.'

'Why are they called silkies?'

'Dunno. Suppose when seals are in the water, they look sleek and shiny, like silk.'

Uncle Vez pulls a face. 'Ugly great brutes. Remind me of giant slugs they do, with their heads waving this way and that.'

'Ugly? Never!' Ted frowns. 'Awkward maybe, on land, but watch 'em swimming, they change. Beautiful they are. Graceful.'

'Like mermaids?'

'Yes,' he smiles at me. 'Just like mermaids. Some say that's what silkies are: mermaids and mermen that try to entice you out to sea.'

'Here we go!' groans Uncle Vez. 'More tall stories.'

Ted ignores him. 'And some say they're ghosts.'

'Whoo, whooo, whoooo!' Uncle Vez raises his arms up and chases Stanika round the yard. Jellico joins in, barking. I tug at Ted's sleeve.

'Are there really such things as ghosts?' I whisper.

Ted looks down at me. 'No. Take no notice of me, Mattie. They're just old wives' tales.'

But I don't mind if there are ghosts, so long as they're nice.

Everyone's going to the Mine Museum but I want to go to the beach.

'You can't go on your own,' says Mum.

'I won't be on my own, I'll be with Will.'

'Who's Will?'

'My friend.'

'Her *imaginary* friend!' grins Dontie.

'He's not imaginary, he's real!'

'I tell you what, I'll come down to the beach with you,' says Mum. 'I could do with a rest. And Stanika can come too.'

But Stanley wants to go to the Mine Museum. And Anika has to go with him.

'Looks like it's just you and me,

Mattie,' says Mum.

There's no sign of Will on the beach. Mum puts her towel down on the sand and lies back with a contented sigh. 'Don't go in the sea without me, Mattie,' she says. And then she falls asleep.

'Want to go swimming?' says a voice at my shoulder. It's Will.

I stare at him in delight.

I'd forgotten how his fair hair flops forward into his brown eyes.

I'd forgotten how bony his elbows and knees are.

I'd forgotten how his ribs jut through his skin like they're trying to break out.

I've forgotten how brown as a berry he is.

'I can't,' I say regretfully.

'Why not?'

'Mum says.'

'Is that your ma?' Will stares at her, lying there, sleeping.

'Yes. She's having a baby.'

'I know. My ma had babies too. Lots of them.'

'Won't your mum be looking for you?' I ask.

'Not any more,' he says and looks sad.

So to cheer him up I say, 'Show me more things?' and we go off and find more rock pools and today he shows me shrimps, and prawns which are bigger than shrimps, and little fish called blennies and gobies which I can't tell apart even though he explains how to.

Then he chases me along the shore with a big piece of soggy wet seaweed which he calls bladder-wrack.

And then I chase him. It's ace.

After that we go down to the water's edge and he shows me how to skim and we have a competition to see how many times we can bounce flat stones across the sea.

Then we have a second round.

Then we have a third.

Finally, by the time we get to the tenth round, I beat him!

'You're a quick learner!' he says.

I can feel myself swelling with pride. I really like Will.

I like him as much as Lucinda.

'Aren't you cold?' I ask. He's dressed the same as yesterday, just a scruffy pair of trousers, tied at the waist with string, nothing else.

'No. I don't feel the cold, me. I like it here on the beach.'

'Me too.'

'I like swimming in the sea.'

'Me too.'

'I *hate* being stuck inside,' he says and his face goes fierce.

'Me too,' I say and I touch his hand and his face goes soft again.

But his hand feels freezing cold to me.

'MATTIE?' I can hear Mum's voice

calling me from up the beach. 'Come here this minute!'

'Race you to my mum!' I shriek and dash off as fast as I can. Behind me, I can hear Will laughing.

Mum is cross with me. 'I thought I told you to stay away from the sea when you're on your own.'

'I wasn't swimming!' I protest. 'And I wasn't on my own. I was with Will.'

'Your imaginary friend?' asks Mum, with her eyebrows raised. 'He doesn't count.'

'He's not imaginary!' I protest, but she's not listening.

When I turn around, Will has disappeared.

Chapter 16

The sun comes out and the sea turns blue like the sky and lots of families come to the beach. Mum stops worrying so much about us getting into danger because there are so many people around. Suddenly there are lots more children to play with. But I like playing with Will best.

He always hides in the caves when there are people about. I think he's a bit shy.

The caves are bigger than they look. I thought they only went back a little way, but Will shows me some secret tunnels that lead right up inside the cliff.

'Where do they go to?' I ask, crouching on my hands and knees in the damp, cold darkness, hoping Mum doesn't find out where I am.

'To the tin mine.'

'I'm glad I'm not a miner,' I say as water drips down my neck. 'I don't like it in here. Let's go back to the beach.' And I crawl out backwards into the sunshine.

I share my lunch with him whenever I can. Sandwiches, crisps, apples. He eats more than I do. Once I brought a pasty down to the beach for us to share and he scoffed the lot.

'Ma used to make these,' he said, gulping down the last bit like a baby seagull. Then he saw my face and said,

'Sorry!'

I didn't really mind. He's my friend.

One day Will takes me to see the seals. We climb up the cliff and follow the path along the top. Then we gaze down into a rocky cove where waves splash against huge boulders which Will says are made of granite.

'There's none there,' I say, disappointed. But then a rock moves and makes its way clumsily down to the sea. Another one follows.

'Camouflage!' I say in delight.

We watch the seals lazing on the rocks below, soaking up the sun. Sometimes they roll over onto their backs with their flippers stuck out as if they're sunbathing.

'Where's their Factor 50?' I ask. 'And their sunhats?' Will looks at me as if he hasn't got a clue what I'm talking about.

Another seal struggles up onto its flippers and waves its head from side to side. Slowly, it shuffles over the rocks and flops headfirst into the water.

'Uncle Vez was right,' I say, disappointed. 'Seals are just big, blubbery slugs.'

But then, before my eyes, the big, blubbery slug changes into a supple, silky shadow that darts swiftly away through the deep, turquoise sea.

'No, Ted was right after all!' I say in delight. 'They're beautiful!'

Will laughs at me, but in a nice way. 'You're not the full shilling, are you?' he asks.

'Yes I am!' I say, though I don't know what it means.

I expect it means he likes me.

Chapter 17

I tell Dontie and V about the seals. The next day they want to go and see them for themselves.

'If you don't take us, I'll tell Mum that you go off on your own,' says V.

'No I don't!' I protest. But in a way, she's right. I go to the beach with them every day but I always go off and play with Will on my own. If anyone else is there, he won't come out.

We go down to the beach to look for Will

and, guess what? He's nowhere to be seen. There aren't many people on the beach today. A cold wind whips my hair into my eyes and the sky is grey.

'Will?' I shout into the cave. I know he's hiding in there, cooped up inside one of the tunnels. 'I'm taking Dontie and V to see the seals. You coming?'

But there's no answer.

Maybe he's sulking because he wants the seals to be our secret. V sniggers and I feel a bit cross. With Will, more than with her. My brother and sister have never met him and they think I'm making him up. I'm not! It's all his fault for hiding away.

'Right then!' I shout into the cave. 'We'll go on our own.'

Dontie, V and I climb back up the cliff and walk along the path, past the old tin mine and the miners' cottages where Will told me he lived.

In the front garden of one them, a baby is sitting in a pram while his mum tries to peg washing out on the line. It's flapping like mad in the breeze. She smiles at us as we go past.

I wonder if it's Will's ma. She looks nice.

Once we've passed the cottages, the path turns a corner and now the wind is really strong. V, who is not very big, is nearly blown off her feet and she shrieks at the top of her voice.

'Wow!' I say, grabbing her just in time. 'Hold on to me.'

We trudge along, heads down, battling against the wind. It seems much further today. At last we come to the top of Seal Cove.

'Here we are.'

'Where are the seals?'

'Down there. Be careful!' I yell as they both peer over the cliff.

'I can't see any,' says V, disappointed.

'There they are! Look!' shouts Dontie, excited.

'Where?'

'There!' says Dontie, pointing.

'I can't see them!' V whines. 'It's not fair.'

'Duh! On the rocks?' Dontie moves a step closer to the edge. 'Open your eyes, stupid!'

'I'm not stupid!' snaps V and takes two steps forward. And wobbles.

Quick as a flash, without thinking, I grab her.

Dontie lurches forward to pull her back too, but it's too late, she's flat on her face beside me, so he misses.

And suddenly, he's gone. And all that is left is a noise.

A scary, scuffling, scrabbling noise.

A slipping, slapping, sliding noise.

Then I hear sticks snapping and stones falling and over and over, my brother's voice calling.

'MATTIEEEE!'

And then...
Nothing.

Chapter 18

'Stay there!' I scream at V and I scramble down the cliff, sliding on my bottom, clinging onto rocks, bushes, scrubby bits of grass, anything.

My heart is thudding so much it feels like it's trying to burst right through my chest and my legs and elbows are skinned, but I don't care.

Near the bottom I can see my brother lying on the rocks, like a broken toy.

'Dontie!' I wail but he doesn't answer.

'Dontie!' I scream and this time seagulls wheel up into the sky, shrieking.

But still my brother lies there like a discarded doll.

First thing I notice: no blood.

Second thing I notice: still breathing.

Dontie is lying on his back on a flat granite rock above what little beach there is. The tide is coming in fast and the sea is swallowing up the sand before my eyes. Soon it will be lapping the rocks.

'Stop messing about, Dontie!' I sob. 'You've got to move.'

But he doesn't answer.

I tug him on the arm.

I pinch him on the cheek.

I flick him on the nose. Hard. He hates that.

I slap him on the face. Twice.

He'd kill me if he knew what I was doing to him.

But he does nothing.

I need to move him. Quick.

Where to?

I can't get him back up the cliff, it's too steep.

I can't get him down on the beach. The sea is too high.

There's a funny noise, part moan, part sob, part whimper.

Not Dontie. Me.

I don't know what to do. There might be something broken. I don't think I should move him. But if I don't and the tide comes in some more, he's going to drown.

All my worry lists have come true.

'MATTIEEEEE!'

I look upwards. V's anxious little face peers down at me from the cliff top.

'GO AND GET HELP!' I yell. 'GET DAD!'

Her face disappears.

I take off my sweatshirt and cover my brother with it. Then I lie down beside him.

One after the other, the seals make their way to the edge of the rocks and slip into the sea.

We're on our own.

Chapter 19

I don't know how long we're there.
It seems like forever.

Suddenly I hear a familiar voice.

'Can't stay there all day. Tide's
coming in.'

'Will!' I jump to my feet, relief flooding
through me.

'Come on. I know a way up top.'

'He can't move.'

'Why not?'

I look at Dontie. He's sitting up, dazed.

'Come on, mate,' says Will, hauling him to his feet.

He gives us a hand-up onto a ledge. Behind it is the dark mouth of a cave.

We follow Will to the back of the cave, to a tunnel. 'Watch your heads!' he warns us.

Inside the tunnel it's pitch dark, freezing cold and soaking wet. Water is dripping down my neck. We squeeze our way through the narrow passage, holding hands all the time, in a chain. First Will, then me, then Dontie.

I can tell that we are going up, up through the rock, up inside the cliff, and I should be scared stiff. But I trust Will. He knows these tunnels like the back of his hand.

Then it becomes too low to stand up

and we get down on our hands and knees and crawl, and that bit *is* scary.

But after a while we can stand up again and it starts to get lighter. At last Will comes to a full stop.

'Look!' he says and points upwards. Above us is a hole. Beyond it is the sky. We've made it.

Will levers himself up through the hole first.

'Where are we?' I ask as he pulls me up. The sky is overcast but the light still blinds me after the blackness inside the cliff.

'Back at the tin mine,' he says. 'We came up through a mineshaft.'

Dimly, I can make out the engine-house and the winding wheel that was used to bring the miners up from underground. I give Will a hand to pull my brother up to the surface. Dontie sprawls on the grass on his back, shielding his eyes from the light.

'DONTIEEE! DONTIEEE! MATTIEEE!'

My head jerks up like a puppet on a wire. Our names are being called, no, *screamed*, so loudly, it seems to bounce off the cliff top and echo out to sea. I blink. A crowd of people is running towards us.

It's the entire Butterfield family, led by V and Jellico. Behind them is Dad, then Mum who is the one shouting out our names, and Uncle Vez and Stanika. Close on their heels come Ted and some men, laden with ropes and pulleys.

All of them to the rescue.

But we don't need them now.

Will beat them to it.

'How did you know?' I turn to him. 'How did you know we needed you?'

But he's gone.

Chapter 20

Dontie gets put to bed in the farmhouse under a nice soft duvet. We all stand round his bed while the doctor checks him out.

'You'll survive,' he says when he's finished poking and prodding my brother. 'Nasty bump on the head but you've got a thick skull. No harm done.'

'You've got your sister to thank for that,' says Mum and she squashes me so hard against her tummy I swear I can feel the baby kicking me in protest. 'She rescued you. I can't bear to think what might have happened if she'd left you there with the tide coming in.'

'V ran for help,' I say and V beams proudly as Mum squashes her too.

'How did you know the way up through the cliff?' asks Dad.

'Will showed us.'

There's silence in the room. But everyone is staring at me and it's a really loud silence, so loud I can hear what they are thinking.

'Tell them, Dontie,' I say. 'Tell them how we held hands and Will led the way.'

Dontie rubs his head, confused. 'I'm sorry, Mattie, I can't remember a thing.'

You can see he's telling the truth.

'Plenty of rest, that's what he needs

now,' says the doctor, snapping his bag shut, and then he's gone.

Everyone is still staring at me.

'Well, I think you're a very brave girl,' says Mum finally.

'I think you're a star,' says Dontie.

'I think you're a megastar,' says V.

'I think you're a hero,' says Dad.

'A heroine,' corrects Uncle Vez.

'Superman,' says Stanley.

'Man,' echoes Anika.

I smile at them all. I suppose I did OK for a Penelope Panic Pants.

It's nice that they think I'm brave.

But actually, I'm not.

It was Will who was brave, not me.

Chapter 21

Our tent is packed up and we're sitting on our luggage in the farmyard. It's the end of our holiday.

'Don't budge!' warns Mum. 'We don't want to miss that bus. If we miss the bus, we'll miss our train.'

Then she takes Stanika off to the dodgy loos for the last time, adding, 'I won't miss the toilets, that's for sure.'

Dontie starts a game.

'We'll miss the bus, we'll miss the train,

but we won't miss the toilets.'

'We'll miss the bus, the train and the toilets, but we won't miss Greta the pig,' says V, picking up on it fast.

'We'll miss the bus, the train, the toilets and Greta the pig, but we won't miss the rain,' says Uncle Vez, joining in.

This is my sort of game. But I don't feel like playing.

Because *I'm* going to miss my friend Will. Big time. And I haven't even said goodbye to him. Or thanks.

I haven't seen him since he rescued Dontie. Mum hasn't let us out of her sight.

I have written it on my Worry List in big black capitals.

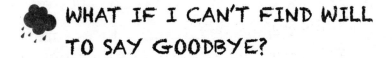 WHAT IF I CAN'T FIND WILL TO SAY GOODBYE?

But now it's too late. I want to go down to the beach just one last time, to see if he's there, but Mum won't let me.

'You can say goodbye to him here,' she'd said. Which shows she thinks I'm making him up.

'Cheer up, Mattie,' says Dad, but I can't. 'Oh, I nearly forgot!' He hands me a postcard. 'I bought you this for Grandma and Granddad the day we went to the Mine Museum. It's too late to post it now. Give it to them when you get home.'

The postcard is strange. It's of a very old photograph, so old it's brown and crinkly. It's a picture of men who worked in the mine a hundred years ago. They're wearing helmets and their faces are streaked with dirt.

'They were the shift who got killed when the mine collapsed,' explains Dad. 'They were trapped underground.'

Trapped underground in the darkness. A shudder runs through me.

'Terrible time that was.' Ted has come up behind me. 'My granny was a girl when it happened. She told me about it. '

'Did all these men die?' I ask.

'Afraid so. See if I can remember who they were.'

Ted sits down next to me and looks at the postcard. Then he reels off the names like he's learned them by heart.

'Tommy Taylor, Arthur Roberts, Jeremiah Scannell ... he left a widow and seventeen children, he did...

'Francis Keen, Edward Trevorrow, Joseph May ... another big family there...

'Joseph Madden, about
to be married, John Payne and
a father and son, Richard Pentecost...'

He points to a figure on the end of the
front row, smaller than the rest.

'And little William Pentecost, God help
him, the youngest of them all. Only a boy
he was, lived next door to my granny in
the cottages. Played together all day long
on the beach they did, 'til the day he was
sent down the mines alongside his father.

Hated it down there, she said, poor little scrap.'

I peer at the face he is pointing to.

My heart misses a beat.

Will stares back at me, his face grainy, dirty, but unmistakable.

'He could swim like a fish, Granny said. Worse thing was, they recovered all the bodies save his. Terrible to think of a lad like that trapped underground forever.' Ted's face is sad.

'Right then,' says Mum as she comes back from the toilets with Stanika. 'We're ready. Now, where's that bus?'

'Won't be a minute!' I say and dash across the farmyard as fast as I can before anyone can stop me.

Chapter 22

I stop at the top of the cliff and gaze down at the beach below.

It's deserted.

No sign of a skinny, brown boy with sun-streaked hair, searching for food in rock pools.

I bite my lip in disappointment.

But then, far out on the rocks, a movement catches my eye. A lone seal struggles up and stretches its neck.

I scramble down the path, run across

the beach and climb over the rocks towards it. It turns its head to study me, waiting.

The eyes are soft, brown, familiar.

'I knew it was you,' I say and he dips his neck in agreement.

'Thank you,' I say.

Now his neck sways from side to side, like he's saying, 'It was nothing,' and I giggle.

I put out my hand to touch him but he shuffles away slowly to the edge of the rocks. Then he swings around again to look at me once more.

He's waiting for my permission to leave.

He's waiting for me to set him free.

'Go you,' I say softly and he slips into the sea with barely a splash.

I wave goodbye as my silkie swims

gracefully away to freedom.

When I can see him no more I turn and climb back up the path to my family.

At the top of the cliff, I can see someone waiting for me. It's Mum. Against the blue sky she looks like a drawing of a stick person with a tiny bump for the new baby. Everyone else is busy piling their stuff onto the bus.

Now I'm going to get it.

But Mum puts her arm around me and squeezes me gently.

'Said your goodbyes have you?' she asks.

I nod.

'Then it's time to go.'

THE END

My Funny Family –
What Happens Next

My Funny Family Gets Bigger

It's the new school term and, as the baby
in Mum's tummy gets bigger and bigger,
the family begins to plan for Christmas –
making lists and wrapping presents.
But could an unexpected Christmas
gift be just around the corner?